This book is presented to:

Abby

On the occasion of:

Easter

From:

Manna

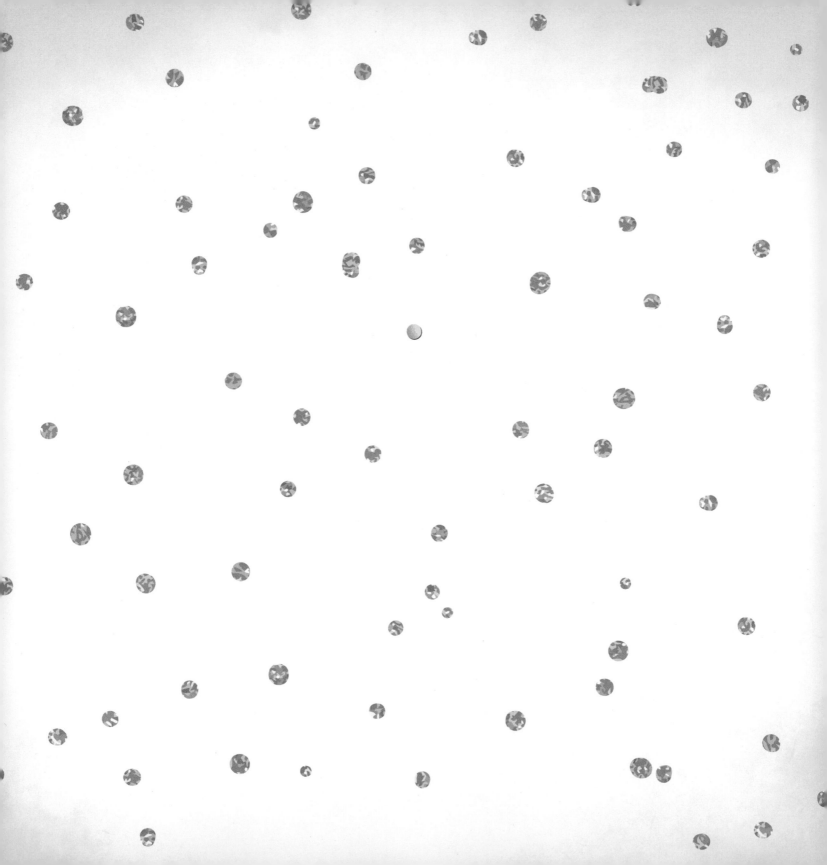

Roxy the Ritzy Camel

Anthony DeStefano

Illustrated by
Richard Cowdrey

HARVEST HOUSE PUBLISHERS
EUGENE, OREGON

This book is for my longtime friend and colleague, Janet Morana.
–Anthony DeStefano

For Cindy, who loves her bling, but loves Jesus more!
–Richard Cowdrey

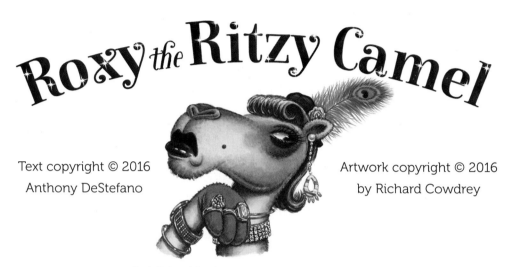

Roxy *the* Ritzy Camel

Text copyright © 2016
Anthony DeStefano

Artwork copyright © 2016
by Richard Cowdrey

Published by Harvest House Publishers
Eugene, Oregon 97402
www.harvesthousepublishers.com

ISBN 978-0-7369-6634-4

For more information about Anthony DeStefano, please visit his website:
www.anthonydestefano.com

Cover and interior design by Left Coast Design, Portland, Oregon

Printed in China

16 17 18 19 20 21 22 23 24 / LP / 10 9 8 7 6 5 4 3 2 1

It is easier for a camel to go through the eye of a needle than for someone who is rich to enter into the kingdom of God.

Mark 10:25

Note: As far back as the ninth century, the Eye of the Needle was thought to be a small stone gate in Jerusalem that opened after the main gate was closed at night. A camel could pass through this smaller gate only if it stooped low and had its baggage removed.

Roxy the camel
Was ritzy and vain.
She thought she was gorgeous
But really was plain.

Just a tad snooty,
And just a bit plump,
The fine food she ate
Gave her quite a big rump.

But oh, was she ritzy!
As ritzy as could be.
She loved jam and crumpets
And afternoon tea.

With jewels round her neck
And earrings of pearls
And ruby-red lipstick
Like all the rich girls,

She had a big mansion,
A butler and maid,
A wardrobe of furs,
Fancy leather, and suede.

She lived in a desert,
As all camels do,
Which can be delightful
But difficult too.

There's sand in the desert—
No flowers or trees.
No cool, windy weather,
Not even a breeze.

And worst thing of all,
No clouds fill the sky.
So rain never falls,
And everything's dry.

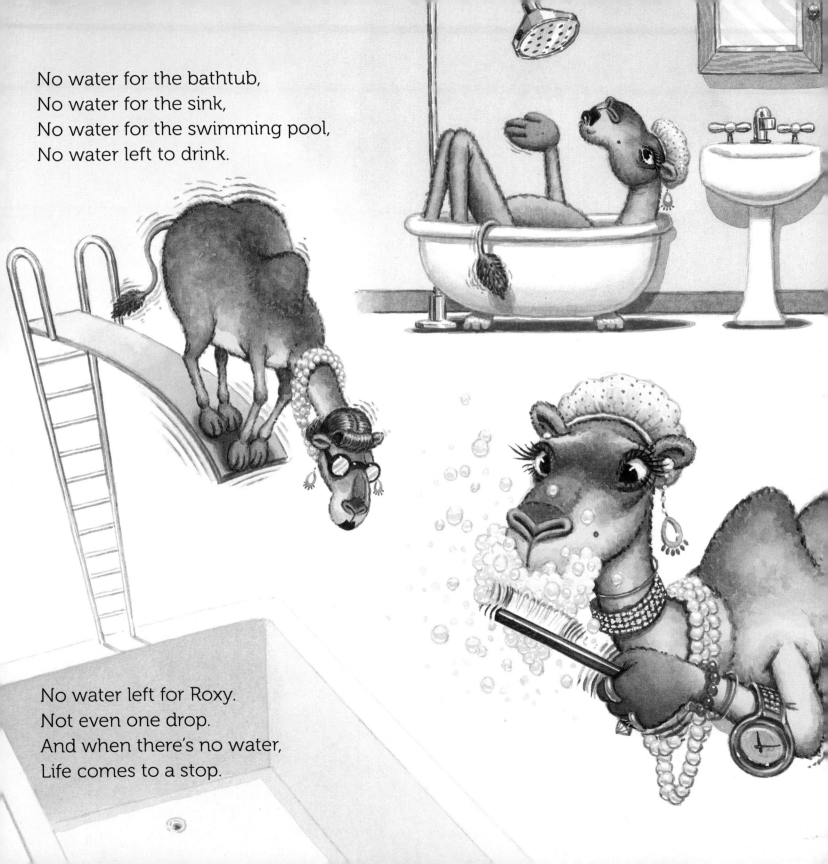

No water for the bathtub,
No water for the sink,
No water for the swimming pool,
No water left to drink.

No water left for Roxy.
Not even one drop.
And when there's no water,
Life comes to a stop.

So Roxy decided
To find a new home,
To leave her big mansion
And go off alone.

She'd heard of a city
All her life long,
Ruled by a king,
Wise, good, and strong,

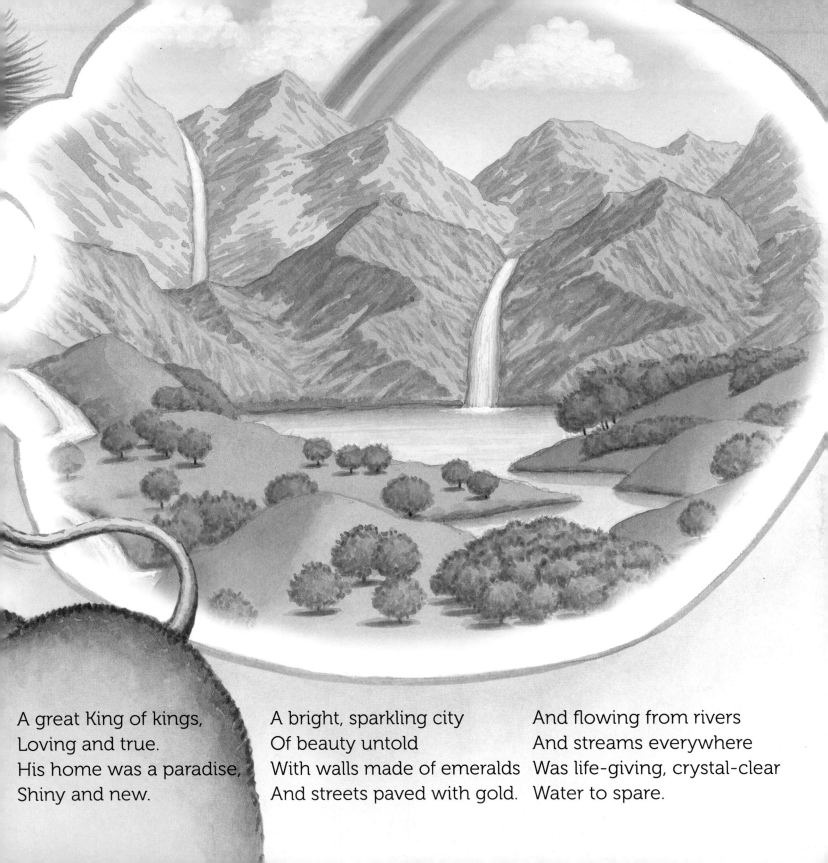

A great King of kings,
Loving and true.
His home was a paradise,
Shiny and new.

A bright, sparkling city
Of beauty untold
With walls made of emeralds
And streets paved with gold.

And flowing from rivers
And streams everywhere
Was life-giving, crystal-clear
Water to spare.

But before Roxy left
She packed and got dressed.
And being so ritzy,
She just packed the best.

Scarves made of silk,
Hundreds of shoes,
A roomful of pocketbooks...
So hard to choose!

Coco-Camel makeup,
Calvin Camel jeans,
Bags of gold and diamonds—
Enough for several queens.

She loved all her riches
With all of her heart,
And tying them round her,
She turned to depart.

But out in the desert
There's not any road,
And traveling's not easy
With such a big load.

So Roxy grew tired
And weary and weak.
Her mouth was so dry,
She barely could speak.

For forty long days
And forty long nights,
She carried her bundles
With no hope in sight.

By the time she arrived
At the great city's wall,
She felt so exhausted,
She thought she would fall.

But at least she was here
And set to go in!
Her wondrous new life
Was about to begin!

She ran to the gate
And tried to go through,
But the hole was too tiny—
It just wouldn't do!

She pushed and she wiggled
Without any luck.
She squeezed in so tight,
Her bottom got stuck!

She just couldn't fit,
There wasn't a doubt.
So Roxy reluctantly
Backed her way out.

"It's not right and not fair!"
She moaned and she cried.
"This gate wasn't made
For a camel so wide."

WELCOME

But just at that moment,
From way up above
There came flying downward
A little white dove.

The dove fluttered softly
Around Roxy's head,
Then finally landed
And quietly said,

"Listen, my friend,
I tell you, it's true,
You're too overloaded
With bags to get through.

"So lighten your load by
Sharing your things.
Give away all your jewels
And your gems and your rings."

"What's that, you say?"
The shocked camel said.
"Give away all my things?
I'd rather be dead!

"No, thank you," said Roxy.
"I'll try it once more,
But this time I'll charge
Like a big, wild boar."

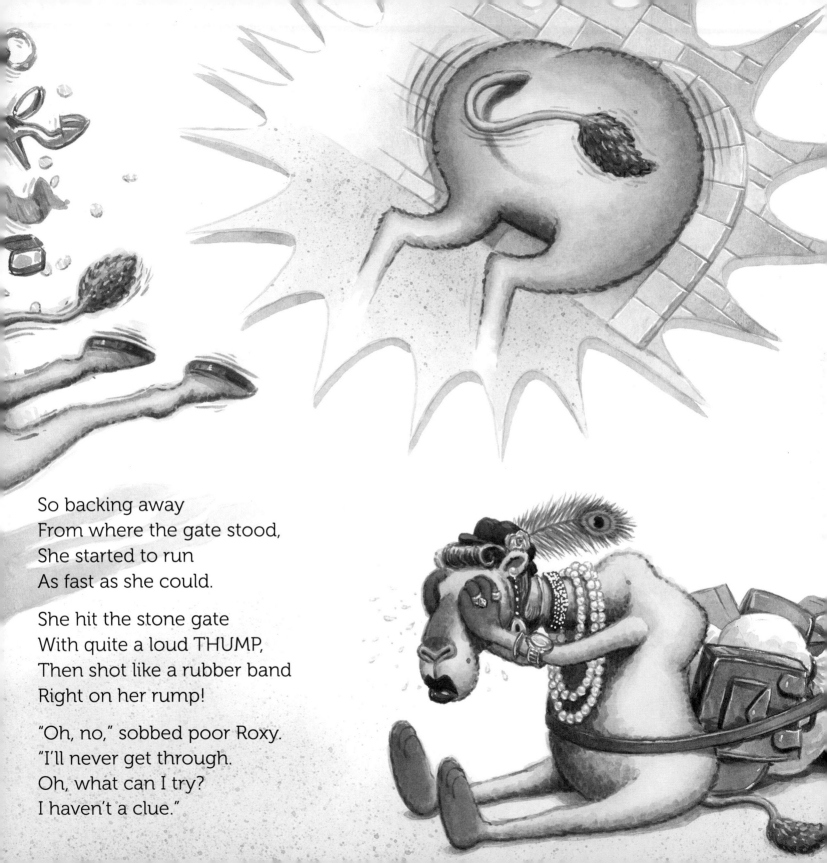

So backing away
From where the gate stood,
She started to run
As fast as she could.

She hit the stone gate
With quite a loud THUMP,
Then shot like a rubber band
Right on her rump!

"Oh, no," sobbed poor Roxy.
"I'll never get through.
Oh, what can I try?
I haven't a clue."

"Please listen to me,"
Repeated the dove.
"Please do what I say,"
He asked her with love.

"Your riches don't matter.
Their value's not great.
They're useless to you
Once you pass through this gate.

"It's nice to have things,
And they can be good
As long as you treat them
The way that you should.

"You're being too selfish
And not very smart
To love them with all of your soul
And your heart.

"That kind of love is
For heaven alone.
It's not for the things
That you buy or you own!

"So share all your things
Or give them away.
Listen, and you'll be so happy today!"

Down deep in her heart,
The rich camel knew
She loved her possessions too much—
It was true.

And so she decided
To give it a try,
To take all her treasures
And kiss them goodbye!

She made up her mind
To give up her things,
To put all her faith
In the great King of kings.

So down by the road,
She gave to some mules
Her bags filled with gold
And big, sparkling jewels.

She gave to a fox,
Whose fur was a mess,
Her frilly, white socks
And bright, silky dress.

She gave to a slow
And lonely old tortoise
A diamond tiara
That really looked gorgeous.

She gave to some snakes—
Not known for their looks—
Her collection of hats
And posh pocketbooks.

She gave to a lion
Off taking a snooze
Her bows and her braids
And boxes of shoes.

And when she was done,
She noticed that she
Was so much more happy
And so much more free.

Her heart felt so light,
Her soul felt so bright,
She danced and she floated
Like a butterfly in flight.

Then squinting her eyes
She started to trot.
She said to the dove,
"Let's give this a shot!"

She rushed to the gate,
But still it was tight.
She squished and she pushed
With all of her might.

The little dove just watched,
Then flew around and said,
"Try bowing down and going in
On bended knees instead.

"That's the way!" he cheered her.
"You're almost free and clear!
All you animals get behind
And push her on her rear!"

They pushed and shoved together.
They poked and prodded too.

POP!

Then suddenly there was a POP,
And Roxy made it through!

Once inside the city,
The camel looked around.
She couldn't breathe or quite believe
The beauty she had found.

Valleys, vineyards, mountains, trees
Rising in the air,
Lakes and rivers, streams and seas—
And water everywhere!

Best of all, the King came forth
And welcomed Roxy in.
He said to her, "Well done, my friend.
Your joy can now begin!

"No more thirsting, no more tears,
No more pain or strife.
In this land of happiness
Forever you'll have life."

And all the city gathered round
And gave a thunderous cheer!
For Ritzy Roxy—rich with love—
At last had made it here!

The end.